FAIRY STORIES
STORYBOOK AND KALEIDOSCOPE VIEWER

adapted by Sarah Heller
from original stories by Laura Driscoll and Kirsten Larsen
illustrated by Judith Holmes Clarke
and the Disney Storybook Artists

Reader's Digest
Children's Books

Pleasantville, New York • Montréal, Québec • Bath, United Kingdom

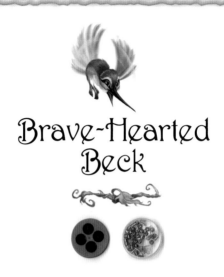

Brave-Hearted Beck

Beck is an animal-talent fairy. She can speak the language of any creature in Never Land. Sometimes she even understands baby animals that don't chatter and chirp yet. Beck feels what they are feeling.

One morning, Beck tries to talk to a baby raccoon who is sad and scared. Beck knows how to cheer him up. She teaches him a game called "find the fairy." As Beck darts and dashes around him, the raccoon begins to laugh. Soon he trusts Beck.

"I want to go home," the little raccoon tells her.

"What does home look like?" asks Beck.

Tearfully, the raccoon holds up some mint that he found in a fairy garden.

Disk 1
1

When Beck explains to her friends that the raccoon is lost, a forest-talent fairy helps them find an oak tree near some wild mint. And there they found the raccoon's family.

"Thank you, Beck," says Mother Raccoon.

On the way to tea, Beck says hello to the moles. "Good day, Sir," says Grandfather Mole. He is quite blind and cannot see that Beck is a girl fairy. It makes her laugh and she continues on her way.

2 Suddenly, a hummingbird comes zooming toward her. "Twitter!" scolds Beck when she gets her breath back. Twitter is a nervous young hummingbird. Often, Beck is the only animal-talent fairy who can calm him down.

"Beck, the chipmunks are stealing," cries Twitter. "They gather berries and seeds, but they don't eat them, they just take them away!"

Beck teaches Twitter that chipmunks store their food for the winter in their burrows.

"Well, okay then," says Twitter.

"I'll see you later," Beck tells him, then she flies to the tearoom. There, Beck notices something unusual. Many fairies are covered in berry juice.

"Berries are falling from the sky!" says Fawn.

Just then, Twitter appears at the window, tapping nervously. "It's an emergency!" cries the young bird. Beck is sure he's overexcited until Twitter mentions berries.

"Okay, Twitter," says Beck. "Show me where the trouble is."

Beck quickly follows her friend to a blackberry bush. Birdie, a hummingbird elder, is directing the birds to fling blackberries at chipmunks.

3

"Birdie, what did the chipmunks do?" asks Beck.

"They stole a hummingbird nest!" cries the angry bird.

Beck is sure Birdie must be wrong. She flies to the chipmunk den to sort it out.

"We did no such thing!" Uncle Munk, the chipmunk elder, declares. "But now those birds are in for a battle."

Oh dear, thinks Beck. She quickly arranges an umbrella exchange with the garden fairies. *At least we'll be protected*, thinks Beck. As she heads back toward the battle, berry juice splatters on her flower-petal umbrella. "And just in time, too."

Back in the forest, the chipmunks decide to dig under the blackberry bush to uproot it. While digging, they make a mess of the mole tunnels. Grandmother Mole is angry at the chipmunks. She decides that the moles will join the hummingbirds. Other birds help, too. Soon Pixie Hollow is raining berries.

Even Grandfather Mole gets hit in the crossfire. "My, what large raindrops," he says. "I'll need my hat for weather like this."

Beck has to do something. She tries to talk to the chipmunks. "Can't you just tell the hummingbirds that you didn't take the nest?" she asks Uncle Munk.

"They don't believe us. They just keep attacking."

"And the mice have been scared, too," a young chipmunk named Nan tells Beck. "Now they're going to help us gather the fallen berries and throw them back at the birds."

The chipmunks hurry to battle the hummingbirds, but young Nan is scared. Beck sees a hollow log.

"Come with me, Nan," she tells the chipmunk. "We'll be safe in here."

Just then, Beck notices Twitter trying to dodge the berries. He looks frightened.

"Twitter! Come in the log!" calls Beck.

6 The hummingbird lands quickly. "It's hard to fly out there," he says. His wing is covered in berry juice.

Nan is nervous. When Twitter sees her, he looks at Beck in surprise.

"Twitter, this is my good friend Nan," says Beck. "You know, you two have the same favorite game."

"We do?" asks Nan.

"Hide-and-go-seek?" asks Twitter.

Now Nan is smiling. She loves to play games. So does Twitter. In no time, they are all having fun together in the hollow log.

I wish Uncle Munk and Birdie could get along this easily, thinks Beck.

Beck is wondering what to do when she sees a friend in trouble. Terence, a dust-talent sparrow man, is carrying a large container of fairy dust. He's having a hard time dodging berries.

"Oh, no!" cries Beck as she watches a large berry hit Terence. He loses his balance and falls, spilling fairy dust onto the forest floor. Quickly, Beck flies to help. "Are you okay?" she asks.

Terence licks the berry juice dribbling down his chin. "I'm okay, but I'm not so sure about them," says Terence. He's watching the ants, worms, and spiders that are coated with fairy dust. They are floating happily in the air.

Beck laughs. "At least someone's having fun," she says.

Suddenly, Beck's animal sense tells her something's wrong. It's Twitter and Nan.

They're in trouble and she has to find them fast. There is a hawk perched on the hollow log. Beck can sense the younglings trapped inside. "Don't worry!" she calls to them. "I'll get help."

Bravely, Beck flies through the berry battle to get the attention of Birdie and Uncle Munk. "A hawk! A hawk!" she cries. When the two sides stop fighting, they finally see Nan and Twitter trapped in the log.

Beck flies in front of the hawk, trying to get him away from the younglings. The hummingbirds join Beck, but the hawk does not leave.

Then the chipmunks jump on the hawk's back. He turns to throw them off.

While he's occupied, Uncle Munk comes to the rescue.

"Hurry, you two! Get moving!" he calls. Twitter takes Uncle Munk's advice and flies out fast. Twitter hovers near the log's opening, trying to get Nan to leave, too. But Nan is too frightened.

Birdie has a good idea. She pretends to have a broken wing. When the hawk goes after her, Uncle Munk rescues Nan. Birdie flies to safety and the surprised hawk flies away.

"You did it!" cries Beck. "You worked together."

Birdie looks at Uncle Munk. They are both happy to have Twitter and Nan safe again.

"Can you stop fighting now?" asks Beck.

"If the chipmunks return the nest," answers Birdie.

Uncle Munk looks angry again. "We never stole your nest!" he insists.

Before they can start fighting again, Grandfather Mole strolls by. "Good day, Sir!" he greets Beck. All of the forest creatures stare at Grandfather Mole. He is wearing a very strange hat. It is the missing nest!

Suddenly, Twitter and Nan burst out laughing. All of the forest creatures join them. "Finally," cheers Beck, "the berry battle is over!"

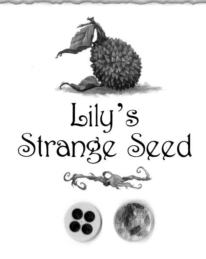

Lily's
Strange Seed

Lily is a garden-talent fairy. She lives in the magical land of Pixie Hollow, just beyond the waterfall in Never Land. Lily loves her garden. She can sense when her plants are happy. When they need care, she knows just what to do.

One morning, when her garden is peaceful and quiet, Lily lies in the cool grass. Some grass blades are racing to grow. Lily holds her breath. Who will win?

"Hiya, Lily!" interrupts a visitor.

Lily leaves the race with a sigh. "Hello, Iris."

Iris is also a garden-talent fairy, but she does not have a garden. Instead, Iris draws and writes about plants in a big book. She visits other garden fairies and gives advice.

"My, your buttercups are beautiful, Lily!" Iris says with a smile. "But they could be larger. And your

snapdragons need manners. If you pinch
their leaves…"

Lily doesn't feel like listening to Iris's
advice today.

"I'd love to chat, Iris," says Lily. "But I'm off
to the forest."

As Lily flies away, she feels guilty about
putting Iris off. But then, she gets caught up in
the mood of the forest. She listens to the birds
singing, and watches the animals playing.
Suddenly, a squirrel rushes by and drops something.

Disk 1

(1)

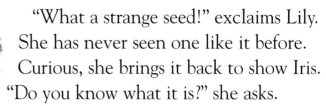

"What a strange seed!" exclaims Lily. She has never seen one like it before.

Curious, she brings it back to show Iris. "Do you know what it is?" she asks.

"Nope," she answers, then reaches for her plant book. "But let me check."

A water-talent fairy named Rani stops by. She has never seen anything like it either.

"I think I will plant the strange seed," says Lily. "When it grows, we'll know what it is."

Over the next few days, Iris helps Lily. Together, the fairies water and feed the soil with chopped vegetables. They talk to the seed.

②
"It sprouted! It sprouted!" calls Iris one morning.

Lily flies over to see a rather brown and sticky seedling.

"What is that ugly weed?" calls a fast-flying talent fairy named Vidia. "You should pull it up, Lily."

"It's not a weed!" cries Iris.

"It's a special new plant," adds Lily, for she can sense that it is true.

However, the other fairies and sparrow men do not share Lily and Iris's joy for the strange plant. As it grows, it gets uglier. Even Lily's good friend Tinker Bell mistakes the strange plant for a monster. Lily has to stop Tink from attacking. "Are you sure it's not a monster, Lily?" Tink asks again.

One morning, Lily smells something terrible in her garden. She follows the awful scent to her new plant. "Oh!" cries Lily in surprise when she sees the droopy white flowers that have blossomed.

Soon many fairies and sparrow men from all over Pixie Hollow arrive with clothespins on their noses. "That stink is ruining breakfast," complains a baking-talent fairy named Dulcie.

Lily hands out lavender flowers to help cover the bad smell. Suddenly, she hears a loud buzzing.

"Wasps!" cries Iris. The fairies dive under bushes. Wasps cover the new flowers. It is very scary. A wasp sting is a terrible danger.

Luckily, Beck and Fawn, two animal-talent fairies, see the swarm and come to rescue their friends.

Riding on the backs of ravens, Beck and Fawn urge the birds to peck and caw until the wasps fly away.

For the next few days, Lily has a hard time. Fairies are afraid to come to her garden. Lily watches for wasps. She gathers more lavender to cover the bad smell.

"What will happen when the lavender runs out?" worries Lily.

"What will happen if the wasps come back?" worries Iris.

"Achoo!" One morning Lily wakes up sneezing. As she flies to her garden she notices pink dust covering everything in Pixie Hollow. *Pollen*, thinks Lily. When she sees the cloud of pink surrounding her new plant, she feels her heart sink.

"Achoo! Achoo!" Everyone in Pixie Hollow is allergic.

"I can't fly fast with this sticky pollen in my wings," pouts Vidia.

"The pollen is getting mixed up with the fairy dust," says a dust-talent sparrow man named Terence.

The fairies are having trouble with their magic. They are sick and grouchy. They all blame Lily's plant.

Lily is sad. She doesn't want the fairies to be angry, but she cannot stand the thought of cutting down any plant, even one that causes so much trouble.

Iris comforts her. "I know this plant is special. It has given me a true friend…you."

"Oh, Iris!" Lily gives her a big hug. "That makes me happy, too."

That evening, Lily sits with her plant. Pollen blows in her nose and she sneezes. "You are very difficult," she tells the plant. "But still I want to protect you. I sense a great secret. Do the other plants know what you are?"

Lily looks at the flowers and the berries. They are leaning in and around the strange plant. "They like you," Lily says. "So you must be good."

Just then, a breeze lifts Lily's wings. The buttercups, clover, and lavender perk up. "What is it?" Lily wonders.

Soon raindrops begin to fall. Lily watches the pink pollen wash away. "Now my friends will feel better again," she smiles happily.

That night Lily sleeps peacefully. Then, in the middle of the night, there is a loud sound. One of Lily's best friends, Bumble the bee, is banging on her window. "What is wrong now?" Lily worries.

Lily hears a cry for help and quickly follows Bumble to her garden. She finds Pell and Pluck, two harvest-talent fairies. Their wings are glued in the sap of the strange plant. Luckily, Tinker Bell and Rani are there to help. Rani warms some water and Lily and Tink wash Pell and Pluck free from the sap.

6

"We heard an owl," says Pell.

"We could have been eaten by a hawk," adds Pluck.

Soon an angry crowd gathers. Iris and Tinker Bell stand with Lily to guard the plant. The other garden-talent fairies back them up. "This is Lily's garden. She has a right to plant what she wants."

Other fairies do not agree.

"Pell and Pluck could have been eaten by an owl," says Fawn. "Wasps may return."

"I had a terrible headache from the pollen," says a sparrow man.

"That plant is ugly, smelly, and dangerous," says Vidia. "We should cut it down!"

Only Queen Clarion can stop the fighting. "I will listen to everyone and make a decision about Lily's plant tonight," she tells them.

Lily has never felt so terrible. All day she worries about her plant. When Lily notices a golden fruit beginning to grow, she tries to hide it. She does not want the plant to cause any more trouble.

"I know this plant belongs in my garden," Lily explains that evening. "The flowers nearby would not be happy and healthy if it were a weed. And I just sense that it is important."

7 "Lily's right!" cries Iris. She holds up a golden fruit. "Her plant is special. It's the only Ever Tree!"

Iris opens her book to show Queen Clarion the story she found. Fairies gather around to see. "Once Never Land was covered with Ever Trees but lava from a volcano destroyed them. The tree grows golden fruit," Iris explains. "If you pick one, another grows in its place."

All of the fairies want a taste. Lily is happy to share. Her Ever Tree is covered with fruit now and it is delicious! "A special tree," says Lily. "But nothing is more special than Iris's garden. She has every plant in Never Land in

8 the pages of her book."